Frosted Sugar Charms

A SHORT SECOND CHANCE MAGICAL ROMANCE

CORAL COVE
BOOK NINE

JAX WILDER

Frosted Sugar Charms© 2025 by Jax Wilder

Published by Rainbow Quartz Publishing

RQPublishing.com

RainbowQuartzPublishing@gmail.com

AuthorJaxWilder.com

Edmonds, WA 98026

Cover design by Miranda Townsend

Edited by Miranda Townsend

First Edition: 2025

Disclaimer: The information contained in this book is for educational and informational purposes only and is not intended as health or professional advice. The author and publisher are not liable for any damages or negative consequences from any action, application, or preparation to any person reading or following the information in this book. References are provided for informational purposes only and do not constitute endorsement of any websites or other sources. Readers should be aware that the websites listed in this book may change.

It's never too late to make your dreams come true.

CHAPTER 1

Zuri

Taking over *Rainbow Bites* was supposed to be a dream come true. And maybe it would be—once I finished scrubbing the lingering smell of peppermint oil out of the walls and threw out the tacky old signage left by Mrs. Claudette. I mean, I loved the woman. She'd watched me grow up, selling me gumdrops for a penny when I was barely tall enough to see over the counter. But her taste? Eccentric at best.

I glanced around at the jars of sweets, colors stacked in neat layers of pastel blues, pinks, and yellows. They were charming in a Coral Cove kind of way—nostalgic, comforting—but it still didn't feel like mine. Not yet.

Just as I was mentally planning a redesign, the

door chimed, and Serena waltzed in, all grace and energy, as if she'd rehearsed her entrance. I didn't even need to turn around to know she'd be dressed to impress, even for a casual candy shop visit. My sister didn't know what "casual" was.

"Good morning, Queen of Sweets," she announced, grinning as she tapped her sunglasses up to rest on her head.

"Hello to you, too, Miss 'Coral Cove Is A Dating Desert,'" I said, smirking as I rearranged a display of lollipops. "How's the search for Mr. Right Now going?"

"Oh, don't even start with me." She let out a dramatic sigh, sliding onto the stool by the counter. "Let me just tell you that the options in this town are bleak. Grim. Like, *post-apocalyptic romance novel* kind of bleak. You know, where the heroine is reduced to dating zombies?"

I laughed, wiping my hands on my apron as I leaned against the counter across from her. "Come on, Serena. It can't be that bad. Maybe you're just... swiping too much?"

She gave me a look that could curdle milk. "That's the thing, Zuri. It's not just the swiping; it's the whole town! I swear, half of Coral Cove is still pining over high school sweethearts, and the other half...well, I think the best way to say it is that they've really *settled* into themselves."

"Maybe you need to raise your standards. Or lower them," I teased, tapping my chin thoughtfully.

"Oh, like you're one to talk!" she shot back. "You're the one who had that whole *tortured artist* phase with Brandon. Remember him?"

I groaned. "Yes, thank you very much for reminding me about *that*."

"Oh, come on! You two were inseparable! Mr. 'I Only Drink Cold Brew and Think Society's Just One Big Conspiracy'?" She rolled her eyes, still laughing. "I could've slapped the angst off his face if you hadn't dumped him first."

"Fine, okay. I'll admit I've had my share of questionable taste in men," I conceded, grimacing. "But what about you and that jazz drummer? The one who went by the name 'Chaz'?"

"Excuse me, that was college," she shot back, feigning outrage. "And we don't speak of the drummer incident. Ever."

We both broke into laughter, loud enough that I almost missed the couple browsing in the corner. They glanced over, smiling, and I waved, mouthing, "Sorry!" I loved that in Coral Cove, everyone was nosy and invested. Half the town would know what we were talking about by noon, and that was part of the charm. There was comfort in knowing you'd never be alone in a place like this.

"So what are you really doing here, Serena? I know you didn't just come to grace me with your beautiful complaints."

She leaned forward, propping her chin on her hand and giving me that look—curious, amused, and just a little nosy. "Well, partly, yes. And I wanted a peek at what you've done with the place."

I swept my arm around dramatically. "Welcome to *Rainbow Bites*. Your one-stop shop for all things sugar and nostalgia. Minus the vintage wallpaper I still need to peel down."

Serena raised an eyebrow, eyeing a particularly garish framed print on the wall of a candy cane garden. "It's... colorful."

"Exactly. So, what do you think? You approve of my little shop?"

"I approve... but it needs more of you. Less Mrs. Claudette." She gave me a pointed look. "You'll get there, though. I know you."

Her words filled me with a warmth that wasn't just from the candy display lights. Sometimes, her encouragement slipped in at the most unexpected times, and this time it hit right.

"Thanks, Serena," I said softly. "I just… I don't know, it feels weird to be back here, trying to run a place that has so many memories. Good memories, but still."

"That's the beauty of it," she replied, her voice softening. "You get to make it your own. Coral Cove wouldn't be Coral Cove without a family-owned candy shop, and I can't think of anyone better to run it than you."

I felt my cheeks flush. I remember the last time I'd I was here, before I moved back.

"What's with that look?" Serena asked, grinning.

"Nothing," I replied, swallowing as the feeling faded.

"Yeah, right. You're thinking about him, aren't you?" Serena's teasing grin was almost too much. "What was his name… Brian? Barry? Oh— *Brandon?*"

"Maybe," I muttered, hoping she'd let it drop. But of course, Serena was never one to drop anything when it came to me.

"Ooh, now we're talking!" she said, eyes brightening. "You two were inseparable back then! Ever think about what would've happened if you two had stayed together?"

"Serena!" I hissed, glancing around as if Brandon himself might pop out from behind the counter. "That was ages ago. Besides, people change."

She shrugged, unfazed. "True. But you still think about him, don't you?"

"Maybe a little," I admitted. "It's hard not to when I'm back here. But I don't see the point in wondering about something that's over."

"Maybe it's not as over as you think," she said with a sly grin. "Why not give him a call? Just to say hi?"

I rolled my eyes. "Oh, sure, I'll just call him up and say, 'Hi, I've been thinking about you. Want to grab coffee?'"

Serena laughed, but her eyes softened. "Okay, okay. I get it. But if it ever happens that you see him again, maybe don't completely shut down the idea."

I smiled, feeling a little lighter. "I'll keep that in mind."

Just as I was about to change the subject, the door chimed again, and a group of teenagers wandered in, laughing and chattering as they made a beeline for the gummy bears. I watched them for a moment, feeling that odd nostalgia again—a strange mix of missing those carefree days and being thankful I'd grown past them.

Serena and I shared a knowing look, the kind that only sisters could pull off. She tilted her head toward the teens and muttered, "Remember when we used to come in here after school, scrounging for whatever candy we could buy with spare change?"

"Oh, please," I replied, smirking. "You were the one stealing quarters from Dad's glove compartment so we could splurge on sour gummies."

She laughed, unashamed. "Hey, those were desperate times. A girl's gotta have her sugar fix."

As the teens filled their bags and paid at the counter, Serena and I watched them with the kind of fondness only people who'd grown up in the same small town could understand. When they finally left, Serena turned back to me, her expression softer.

"You know, Zuri, I'm proud of you," she said, surprising me. "It takes guts to come back here and take over *Rainbow Bites*. And I think… you're exactly where you're supposed to be."

I swallowed, feeling that familiar lump rise in my throat. "Thanks, Serena. That means a lot."

She grinned, reaching across the counter to

squeeze my hand. "Of course. You're my sister. I've always got your back."

In that moment, I felt the weight of the years between us lift. Maybe I wasn't the same girl who'd left Coral Cove for the big city, and maybe my dreams had shifted since then. But with Serena beside me, laughing and teasing as if we were still kids, I felt ready to embrace the life I'd come back for.

There was a little wooden box on the shelf behind the counter that caught my eye. I'd noticed it the first time I'd walked into the shop, years ago, but today something about it just pulled at me.

"What's that?" Serena asked, nodding toward the box. She could spot a mystery from a mile away.

"No clue," I replied, reaching for it. The wood was polished but worn, and the label—faded and curling at the edges—read *Frosted Sugar Charms*.

Serena gasped, leaning in close to examine it. "Is that some kind of relic? Or is it, like, Mrs. Claudette's emergency sugar stash?"

"Could be both," I said, grinning as I carefully lifted the lid. Inside, nestled in a velvet lining, were little candies, perfectly round and dusted with a fine, frosty coating. They were the kind of candy that looked almost too beautiful to eat, each piece in delicate shades of blue, pink, and lavender.

I picked one up, studying it in the light. "They're... kinda magical-looking, aren't they?"

"Like made with fairy dust," Serena agreed, watching as I turned one of the candies over. "What do they taste like?"

"No idea." I laughed, setting it back in the box. "For all we know, Mrs. Claudette left these here as a retirement prank. Maybe they're decades old."

Serena huffed, crossing her arms. "You're no fun, Zuri. Go on, try one! What's life without a little adventure?"

I paused, feeling a strange pang of nostalgia mixed with a little bit of nervousness. "Fine. But if I end up sick, I'm blaming you," I muttered, popping one of the candies into my mouth.

The taste was subtle at first, but then a wave of sweetness washed over me, like the memory of a long-lost day. For a brief second, I could've sworn I was sixteen again, walking the boardwalk in Coral Cove with Brandon, hand in hand, as if the years hadn't changed anything.

The room started to pulse and sway. It was spinning and I was going to be sick. I reached for the counter but grasped only air. Everything went black.

CHAPTER 2

Zuri

I blinked awake, squinting against the soft glow of morning light spilling across unfamiliar walls. Everything was off—my head, my body, the room. The sheets felt different, thicker and softer than the ones on my bed, and as my eyes adjusted, I took in the grand room around me. Plush carpets, a wall-to-wall window with curtains drawn back, and… was that a fireplace?

Disoriented, I sat up, heart pounding as I tried to get my bearings. The last thing I remembered was being at *Rainbow Bites* with Serena, tasting that frosted candy she'd dared me to try. How had I ended up here? And what was "here," exactly?

The sound of breathing beside me made me jump. I whipped my head to the left, finding a man sprawled on the bed beside me, his dark curls tousled against the pillow, his face angled toward me in peaceful oblivion. But it wasn't just any man. It was Brandon.

For a split second, I thought I might be dreaming, but everything was painfully vivid—the warmth of the sheets, the faint morning light, and Brandon's steady breathing. I couldn't explain it, but somehow, here he was.

I nudged him, shaking him slightly. "Brandon?"

He stirred, groaning as he rolled toward me, his face cracking into a sleepy smile. "Morning, Mrs. Lee," he mumbled, his voice thick with sleep.

"Mrs… Lee?" I whispered, my mouth hanging open. I forced a laugh. "Brandon, you're funny. Did you… move me here last night or something?"

Brandon opened one eye, his brows furrowing as he peered at me. "Are you okay?" he asked, yawning and stretching his arms above his head. "You're acting kind of strange, even for you."

I stared at him, trying to piece together any shred of logic that would make this situation make sense. "Sorry, umm this is a nice bedroom?"

Now he was fully awake, propping himself up on one elbow and giving me a look that was half-amused, half-concerned. "It better be, you picked it out and made me buy all this girly shit."

"I did?"

His eyebrow shot up.

I forced a laugh. "I mean, I did. Of course I did." Gods above I didn't understand what was going on.

"Our anniversary's coming up next week," he said, as if that explained everything. "I thought we were doing the no-surprises thing this year. But if you want to act coy, be my guest."

My head spun. An anniversary? This was either the most elaborate prank Serena had ever pulled or... or something else entirely. And given that Serena hadn't shown a commitment to anything this detailed since the third grade, I doubted she'd put in the effort to set this up.

"Brandon," I said slowly, choosing each word with the care of someone navigating a minefield, "do you remember what happened yesterday? Where I was? Or... or what I was doing?"

He laughed, reaching over to tuck a strand of hair behind my ear. "The candy shop as usual. You came home late, tired but still beautiful as ever." He smiled, clearly enjoying himself. "And we both agreed to be in bed by ten. Which we were, though not exactly sleeping." He wiggled his eyebrows.

My cheeks flushed, my mind racing. *Rainbow Bites*. Right. I'd been there, eating that mysterious candy. But none of this made sense. How did I go from my apartment above the shop to... here?

Desperate to ground myself, I pushed the sheets back and stumbled out of bed, making a beeline for the closet door—where I hoped I might find something, anything, familiar. When I opened it, a flood of designer clothes I didn't recognize greeted me. They were stylish but nothing like what I'd actually wear. Dresses, shoes, and purses that looked like they'd been pulled from a magazine were arranged meticulously, each item lined up as if waiting for inspection.

"Where are you going?" Brandon's voice pulled me back to the room, but I was already halfway to the door, glancing over my shoulder.

"Just... need to clear my head. Be right back!" I called, giving him what I hoped was a reassuring smile as I left the room.

Outside, the hallway was wide and tastefully decorated, with abstract paintings and polished wood accents. There was no doubt about it: this was a life I'd somehow missed out on. I took a deep breath and kept walking, resisting the urge to sprint down the hall as I made my way toward the front door.

Once outside, I searched desperately for a familiar landmark. *Rainbow Bites* was only a ten-minute walk from where I was, so I took off in the general direction, half-jogging, my heart racing as I replayed everything Brandon had just said.

Our anniversary. Married. Life together. It was like some strange alternate reality, and part of me expected to snap out of it any second.

Finally, I rounded the last corner, expecting to see *Rainbow Bites* in its cozy spot. Instead, a sign for *Pawn & Play* greeted me—advertising board games, antiques, and vintage finds. The brightly colored candy shop was gone, replaced with a display of chessboards and board game boxes stacked in the window. I pressed my hand against the cool glass, trying to catch my breath. The reality of this new world hit me like a punch to the gut.

"Hey, need some help?" a woman called from behind me. I turned to see Serena, looking much the same as she had yesterday, though a little more put together. Her eyes sparkled with recognition, and she didn't hesitate to pull me into a hug.

"Oh, thank God, Serena!" I gasped, squeezing her. "You wouldn't believe the morning I've had. I woke up in this strange house, Brandon is there, and everyone thinks we're married!"

Serena laughed, nudging me playfully. "Is this supposed to be news? You know, you're married to a pretty great guy, Zuri. All couples go through rough patches. Whatever's happening, you'll get through it."

"No, I mean, I... I don't *remember* being married," I said, emphasizing the last words as if she'd finally catch on. "I woke up in a strange house, *with Brandon*, who I haven't dated since forever ago, and I still can't make sense of any of this."

But Serena just patted my shoulder like I was the one acting strange. "It sounds like you need a break, Zuri. Clear your head. Maybe try actually talking to Brandon? Work through things?"

Her words hit me hard, and I felt a flicker of shame. Was that it? Had I been some distant wife in this alternate life, to the point where even my own sister didn't believe my confusion?

Resigned, I muttered something about needing

to get home and see Brandon. With each step back toward that sprawling house, my mind kept replaying Serena's advice. *All couples go through rough patches. Maybe I just needed to give it a shot.* After all, if Brandon was still the guy I'd once loved, maybe there was something here worth exploring.

When I stepped back inside, Brandon was waiting in the kitchen, an apron over his clothes as he made breakfast. He looked up and smiled, catching my eye with that same easy grin he'd had since we were teens.

"You okay?" he asked, a hint of concern in his tone. "You seem a little off."

"Yeah, just… a lot on my mind, I guess," I said, trying to ignore the lump in my throat. I passed him a coffee cup—I'd bought two on my walk home. "You're really… sweet, you know that?"

He chuckled, shaking his head. "Wow, Zuri, first a compliment and now coffee? Are you trying to make up for something?"

I laughed, though it sounded a little off, even to me. Brandon was stirring something on the stove, the smell of garlic and rosemary filling the kitchen, as if this version of me was the type who knew how to season a roast, or in this case breakfast. The kitchen itself was just... beautiful. Sleek appliances, granite countertops, and an actual pot rack over the island. Nothing like the tiny setup I had in my apartment above *Rainbow Bites*.

"What's on your mind, stranger?" Brandon's voice pulled me back, his warm, familiar eyes meeting mine. That hint of playfulness in his gaze —it was exactly how I remembered him, a softness that made me feel oddly safe despite everything.

I shrugged, feigning nonchalance. "Just... today feels somehow odd to me. Feels like a dream, you know?"

He smirked, turning to slice the garlic with precision. "Guess that's a good sign? Unless you mean the nightmare kind."

"No, not at all," I said quickly, laughing. I watched him, admiring the ease with which he moved, as if we'd done this countless times before. And maybe, in this life, we had. There was something in the rhythm of the day that was comforting and strangely intimate. He'd crack a joke, I'd roll my eyes, and we'd fall into these easy silences that felt so... normal.

I caught myself watching him longer than I should, noticing the way his shirt pulled slightly across his shoulders when he reached for a spice or the way he squinted just a bit when he laughed at his own jokes. I'd forgotten that about him. The little quirks. And then there was the way he drummed his fingers on the counter when he was lost in thought, a habit that used to drive me crazy but now felt strangely endearing.

The buzz of a phone jolted me, pulling me out of my reverie. I glanced over, expecting to see Brandon's phone, but it was mine—except, of course, it wasn't the phone I was used to. It was sleeker, newer, encased in some fancy, glittering cover that screamed "alternate reality me." A text notification glowed on the screen.

Greg: Miss you, gorgeous. When can I see you again?

I blinked, my stomach twisting. Who the hell was Greg? I almost wanted to ask Brandon, but I felt my cheeks heat as I slid the phone back into my pocket, telling myself I'd deal with that later. Brandon seemed unfazed, still focused on his cooking, so I took a deep breath and tried to shake off the unease.

As we sat down to eat, I forced myself to stay present, to savor each little detail of this surreal reality. Brandon poured a cup of coffee, handing it to me with that charming, slightly crooked smile I remembered so well.

"Remember when we did this all the time?" he asked, his gaze softening. "Just the two of us and a lazy Sunday?"

I nodded, feeling a pang in my chest. "Yeah, it… it feels good."

We talked about the small things, memories we apparently shared in this life—weekends we'd spent hiking, movie nights that turned into popcorn fights, the time he'd surprised me with a last-minute road trip to the mountains. I smiled and nodded along, absorbing the memories as if they were mine.

But then the phone buzzed again. Another message from Greg.

Greg: Can't stop thinking about last night. You're driving me crazy, Zuri.

My heart sank. What kind of person had I become here? I forced myself to set the phone aside and tried to focus on Brandon, who was telling me about an upcoming anniversary trip he'd planned for us. I forced a smile, nodding as if I could picture it, but a sense of guilt crept over me.

Brandon noticed my distraction and reached across the table, covering my hand with his. His touch was warm, grounding. "Hey, you okay? You seem a little distant."

I felt a pang of shame, my mind still flickering to those texts, and nodded quickly. "Yeah, sorry. Just... you know, tired." It was the best excuse I could come up with, and thankfully, he let it slide.

After brunch, he suggested we go for a walk, and I found myself relaxing as we strolled down the quiet neighborhood streets. He slid his arm around my shoulders as we walked, pulling me close, and I didn't resist. There was a part of me that was enjoying this far too much, the comfort and warmth of his presence.

We stopped at a little park, sitting on a bench overlooking a small pond. Brandon was quiet for a moment, then turned to me, his expression serious.

"You know," he said softly, "I was starting to think you wanted a divorce. You've seemed so... far away lately."

I stared at him, feeling my heart drop.

"Divorce? No, Brandon, I'd never… I mean, I don't want that."

He searched my face, and for a moment, it felt like he was really seeing me, seeing all the complicated emotions I was trying so hard to hide. "I don't either," he murmured, brushing a stray hair from my face. "We were good once, Zuri. I know we can be again."

I wanted to believe him. In that moment, I almost did. The ache in my chest felt real, and I could feel myself softening, letting down my guard just a little. But then the phone buzzed again, shattering the moment.

This time, I couldn't ignore it. Brandon looked down at my pocket, eyebrows raised, and I felt the color drain from my face.

"Is everything okay?" he asked, his tone a mix of curiosity and concern.

I forced a laugh, shaking my head. "Just… work stuff," I lied, pulling out the phone. But the screen betrayed me.

Greg: You didn't forget about me already, did you?

. . .

I froze, staring at the message, my stomach twisting. The implication was clear, and I felt a rush of guilt and horror. I'd become someone I didn't recognize —someone who would betray the person she loved.

Without thinking, I typed back a quick response.

Zuri: Can't talk now. With Brandon.

I didn't know why I did it. Maybe some part of me felt like this was my chance to fix things, even if it wasn't really my life. I wanted to see this day through, to feel that connection with Brandon without the taint of something—or someone—else.

"Everything okay?" he asked again, his brow furrowed as he watched me carefully.

"Yeah," I said, trying to keep my voice steady. "Just… distracted, I guess."

He slid an arm around me, and I leaned into him, letting myself believe, even for just a moment, that this was my life. That maybe, in some parallel universe, we'd stayed together and worked through our issues. The thought of it felt both comforting and surreal.

By the time we made it back to the house, the

weight of the day had settled on me, a strange mix of nostalgia, regret, and something bittersweet that I couldn't quite put into words. Brandon put on some soft music, dimmed the lights, and lit a few candles, his gaze holding mine as he took my hand and led me toward the bathroom.

The warm scent of lavender and cedar filled the air as he ran a bath, adding oils to the water as if he'd done it a hundred times before. And maybe, in this life, he had.

Brandon undressed and I took in the sight of him, licking my lips, wanting to taste every inch of him.

As I sank into the tub, he slipped in behind me, his hands sliding over my shoulders as he whispered in my ear, "You know, I missed you. The real you. And tonight… you feel like her again."

I felt a lump form in my throat, his words somehow piercing through the surreal haze of the day. I leaned back against him, his arms wrapping around me as his fingers trailed across my skin, tracing lazy circles that made my heart race.

For a moment, I let myself imagine it was real—that I could wake up tomorrow, and this life would still be here, with Brandon. That I wouldn't have to face the cold, unalterable truth of who I'd apparently become in this reality.

He kissed my shoulder, his breath warm against my skin as his hands roamed my body, cupping my breasts, making me shiver as he whispered my name. I closed my eyes, letting myself drown in the moment, feeling his touch, his warmth, everything I'd missed for so long.

But just as I was sinking deeper, letting myself fall into him completely, everything faded. I felt a sharp jolt, and suddenly, I was back in *Rainbow Bites*, staring at Serena's concerned face as she called my name.

"Zuri? Are you okay?" she asked, her voice laced with worry.

I blinked, the warmth and intimacy of the alternate life fading like a dream, leaving me cold and disoriented in the bright lights of the shop. I swallowed hard, nodding quickly.

CHAPTER 3

Zuri

"Yeah... yeah, I'm fine," I managed, though my voice was hoarse, my heart still racing. As I glanced around the bright, familiar shelves of *Rainbow Bites*, the memory of Brandon's touch lingered on my skin, vivid and electric. But I wasn't fine—*not even close*.

"Zuri?" Serena's voice sliced through my haze of confusion. I looked over to find her staring at me, brows knitted in concern. Before I could think of a reassuring lie, the door chimed, and in walked a tall muscular man, with a full beard, smelling of pine.

He had a jolly smile and the casual charm that made him both oddly endearing. He waved to us, heading straight to the counter.

"Morning, ladies! I'm Alex Clause, my wife is

Lea, she owns the bookstore. I just wanted to come by and say hi, introduce myself to the new owner and maybe grab some of your finest chocolates," he said, tapping the glass. "Just a little something special for Lea."

"Lea, huh?" Serena replied, trying to sound breezy.

I reached for the chocolate assortment, my fingers fumbling slightly as I opened the case. *Get it together, Zuri.* "Nice to meet you, Alex," I managed but my hands shook as I placed the chocolates in a box, forcing myself to focus on each movement to keep my mind from spiraling.

"Zuri," Serena said. "Her name is Zuri."

Alex raised an eyebrow, glancing between me and Serena. "You okay there, Zuri? You look… distracted."

I forced a smile, hoping it didn't look as stiff as it felt. "Just… off my game today, I guess."

He accepted the chocolates. "Well, it's nice meeting you. I'll see you around." Alex gave Serena a quick nod before heading out. I barely had a moment to breathe before Serena turned to me, arms crossed and gaze fixed on me like a laser beam.

"Alright, Zuri. Spill. What's going on?" she

demanded. "One minute, you're talking my ear off, and the next, you're staring off into space like you've seen a ghost."

I took a shaky breath, my fingers absently tracing the countertop. "Serena, it's... it's hard to explain."

"Try me," she said, the teasing spark in her eyes replaced with genuine concern. "Or do I need to call poison control? Was the candy expired?"

I almost laughed, but the urge died on my lips. She was right—I did need to spill. Otherwise, the whole experience would stay bottled up in my head, haunting me every time I closed my eyes. I scanned the shop, making sure it was empty, then took a deep breath and started talking.

"It was... the candy," I said, nodding toward the shelf where the *Frosted Sugar Charms* sat innocently, like they hadn't just changed the course of my life in the most confusing way possible. "I don't know how to explain it, but... when I ate one, it took me somewhere else. Like... an alternate life."

Serena's eyes widened, but she stayed silent, nodding for me to go on.

"When I woke up, I was with Brandon," I continued, barely able to keep my voice steady. "And we were... married. It felt like I'd slipped into another world where he and I had never broken up."

Serena's mouth dropped open, but she quickly closed it, her expression shifting from disbelief to pure fascination. "Wait. So you're telling me... a piece of candy took you into some kind of parallel universe?"

I nodded, feeling the weight of each word as I confessed, "Yeah, and it was so real. Like I'd been living that life all along. We spent the day together, talking, cooking, and... reconnecting, I guess."

She tilted her head, an intrigued smile tugging at her lips. "Oh, reconnecting, huh?" Her eyebrow arched, and she leaned in a little closer. "Like, reconnecting?"

I rolled my eyes, feeling my cheeks warm. "Serena, don't—"

"Oh, I'm just asking," she teased, grinning wider as she leaned against the counter. "You know, 'reconnecting' is such a... flexible word. I'm just curious about the, uh, depth of the connection."

I laughed, trying to fight off the blush creeping up my neck. "It was just... it was intimate, okay? We talked, spent time together, and... things felt real. That's all."

Serena gave me a knowing look, her eyes

sparkling with mischief. "Uh-huh. 'Just talking,' my favorite pastime with a hot ex."

I laughed despite myself, shaking my head. "Fine, there might have been... some chemistry. But that's it!"

Her expression softened, but she kept her playful smile. "Well, whatever 'reconnecting' means to you, I hope you at least enjoyed it."

I sighed, thinking of Brandon's familiar touch, his voice, the way he'd looked at me. "Yeah," I murmured, the memory making my heart ache in a way I hadn't expected. "I guess I did."

Serena nudged me, her voice gentler now. "Then maybe that's a little magic right there." She leaned closer, practically hanging on my every word. "So, you're happy in this other life? You two are, like, crazy in love again?"

My stomach twisted as I remembered the messages from Greg. "Not exactly," I said, voice low. "I... apparently, in that life, I'd been... cheating on him."

Her eyes went wide. "*You?* Zuri, you've never even... you know... cheated before."

"I know," I whispered, the shame heavy in my chest. "And that's the worst part. It made me feel sick—like I was watching some horrible version of myself that I didn't recognize."

Serena chewed her lip, eyes narrowing in thought. "Well... maybe he wasn't the right one for you, even there. Because honestly? Cheating happens when something's broken. Either you fell out of love, or maybe he was... I don't know... horrible to you? Maybe he cheated first?"

I shook my head, unwilling to entertain the idea of Brandon as a monster. "No. I can't imagine that. He was... he was just him, Serena. But maybe you're right. Maybe we broke up for a reason in the real world."

Serena nodded, clearly still trying to wrap her head around everything I'd told her. "Okay. So, if this was some kind of glimpse into a different life, then what's next? Are you... are you going to try the candy again?"

Just then, the door chimed again, and we both turned to see Jake Bennett walking in. He looked around the shop before spotting me, his face lighting up in recognition.

"Zuri! Wow, I didn't know you were back in town," he said, strolling up to the counter. "It's been forever."

"Jake!" I grinned, surprised at how good it felt to see him. We'd gone to high school together, but life had taken us in different directions after graduation. "I didn't know you were still here!"

He laughed, scratching the back of his neck. "Oh, I escaped for a while, but Coral Cove has a way of pulling you back. Actually, Amelia's the one who brought me back—she moved here earlier this year and took over Rewind Rentals."

"Amelia's back? That's amazing! And she's running Rewind Rentals?" I couldn't help but smile. The town's tiny video rental store had always seemed to be on the brink of closing, and the thought of Amelia bringing it back to life made me feel a little more at home.

"Yeah, she's really turned it around," Jake said with a proud grin. "It's like a whole new place. You should check it out sometime."

"Definitely. I'll stop by soon." I felt a little flutter as Jake's eyes lingered on me for just a second too long. I was probably imagining it, but there was a warmth in his gaze that made me wonder.

"Well, don't be a stranger," he said, his smile turning into a half-grin that I remembered from our high school days. "Maybe we could catch up sometime?"

"Yeah," I replied, feeling my cheeks warm. "I'd like that."

"Great," he said, giving me one last smile before he turned to leave. "See you around, Zuri."

The door closed behind him, and I felt Serena's elbow jab my side before I could turn around. "Okay, what the heck is going on with you, girl?" she whispered, eyes gleaming with mischief. "Whatever's going on, I want some of it for myself."

I barely had time to react before she bee-lined for the shelf, snatching the box of *Frosted Sugar Charms* and popping one into her mouth.

"Serena! Stop!" I yelped, reaching out, but it was too late—she chewed the candy slowly, savoring it as she grinned at me with a mischievous glint in her eye.

"Oh, come on, Zuri," she said with a smirk. "What's the harm? You're the one who said it was magical."

I shook my head, half-amused, half-panicked. "I can't believe you just... you're impossible, you know that?"

She gave a little shrug, swallowing the candy with a playful wink. "I know. But if I end up in some fantasy life with an ex, don't come looking for me."

I rolled my eyes, but my heart was pounding as I watched her, a part of me both excited and terrified that I just opened Pandora's box.

CHAPTER 4
Serena

I blinked awake, letting out a soft groan as I tried to shake off the haze of sleep. My apartment seemed dimmer than usual, the morning light filtering through curtains that didn't quite look like the ones I'd hung up. I sat up, rubbing my eyes as I took in the small details around me.

The familiar framed photo on my nightstand was still there, but the frame looked newer, more polished. And the blanket draped over the foot of my bed—wasn't that a different color yesterday? I glanced around, feeling a strange blend of familiarity and foreignness, as if I'd woken up in a dream version of my own apartment.

"Serena, you up?" a warm, familiar voice called from the hallway.

I froze, my heart doing an unexpected flip as the door to my room opened, and there he was—Jamal, his easy smile and dark curls looking every bit as handsome as I remembered. He held a mug of coffee in each hand, one of them sporting bold letters that read, *This Might Be Wine*. His gaze softened as he stepped into the room, his lips quirking up in a smirk as he caught me eyeing the mug.

"Don't worry," he said, winking. "It's coffee. Probably." He crossed the room with a relaxed confidence that made it seem like he belonged here —as if we'd woken up together a thousand times before.

"Morning," I replied, my voice a little shaky as I accepted the mug he handed me, trying to keep my expression casual. But inside, my mind was racing. *Zuri didn't mention it would be this real. How is this so real?*

Jamal settled onto the edge of the bed beside me, his hand brushing mine as he sipped his coffee. "Did you sleep okay?" he asked, his tone warm and easy, as if we'd spent a hundred mornings just like this one.

I nodded, struggling to keep my face composed

as I took in the details—the little crease by his eye when he smiled, the warmth of his hand on mine. It was so vivid, so painfully real, I found myself pinching my arm just to make sure I wasn't still dreaming. The slight sting was all the confirmation I needed.

"Yeah, sorry. Just… surprised. In a good way." I let out a slightly shaky laugh, taking a sip of the coffee. It was rich and perfectly balanced, and I half-expected to wake up any second.

""So, what's on your agenda today, beautiful?" he asked, his gaze softening as he looked at me. "I was thinking we could take a walk downtown, maybe grab lunch at that new taco place you mentioned?"

"Uh, yes," I replied, trying to keep my cool despite the giddiness bubbling up inside me. "That sounds… perfect."

We spent the morning strolling along the downtown of Coral Cove, hand in hand, the ocean breeze brushing past us as seagulls circled overhead. I couldn't stop glancing at Jamal, marveling at how real he felt, how natural it was to walk alongside him. And, somehow, he didn't seem to notice my occasional gawking, too engrossed in telling me about a recent project he'd been working on.

"So, I've been tinkering with this old convertible I bought a while back," he said, gesturing animatedly. "I'm not saying it's ready to go yet, but give me a few weeks, and maybe I'll take you for a spin."

I laughed, feeling a warmth spread through me. "I had no idea you were into cars like that. Do you fix them up often?"

"Every now and then," he replied, giving me a casual shrug. "It's my thing, you know? Like your thing is… what is your thing again?" He shot me a playful grin, nudging me with his shoulder.

I chuckled, feeling the thrill of his attention. "It depends on the day. Today, I think my thing is… spontaneous adventures."

Jamal raised an eyebrow, clearly intrigued. "Oh, really? Well, you're in luck, because I know just the place for a spontaneous adventure."

Before I could ask what he meant, he tugged my hand, leading me toward the dock. We rented a small boat—an adorable, vintage-looking sailboat with faded red paint and charm for days—and, with a little guidance from the staff, we set out onto the calm waters.

Out on the open ocean, everything felt surreal.

The horizon stretched endlessly, a canvas of blue and sunlight, and Jamal sat across from me, his dark curls catching in the breeze as he laughed, the sound filling the air like music. It was the kind of picture-perfect day you only read about in romance novels, and I was living it.

He looked over at me, an amused glint in his eyes. "You're awfully quiet. Something on your mind?"

I hesitated, not sure how to explain the whirlwind of thoughts racing through my head. "Just… I'm really happy to be here," I said, my voice softer than I intended.

A warm smile spread across his face. "Me too," he replied, his gaze holding mine for a long moment. And then, slowly, he reached across the space between us, his hand finding mine. His fingers were warm, his touch both grounding and electric, and I felt my heart skip a beat as he gently stroked the back of my hand.

For a second, the world seemed to narrow down to just us, the steady rhythm of the waves fading as we looked at each other, caught in the quiet intensity of the moment. Jamal's hand moved gently over mine, his fingers warm against my skin, grounding me while sending a thrill through my entire body.

He leaned closer, his lips brushing against mine in a slow, lingering kiss that made me forget everything else—the boat, the water, the whole world.

His hand slipped to the small of my back, pulling me just a little closer as he deepened the kiss, his mouth exploring mine in a way that felt familiar. His fingers traced up my spine, igniting a trail of heat that made me shiver. I could feel his breath mix with mine, each kiss charged with the kind of tension that felt like it had been waiting years to unfold.

I leaned into him, my hand finding its way to the back of his neck, pulling him closer. The boat rocked gently beneath us, but we were too lost in each other to notice. He drew back just enough to look at me, his dark eyes searching mine, a smirk tugging at the corner of his mouth.

"Guess this counts as part of our adventure, huh?" he murmured, his voice low and rough.

I smiled, still a little dazed, my fingers lingering on his chest. "Yeah," I managed, my heart racing. "I'd say so."

Without another word, he closed the gap between us, his kisses growing more urgent, his hands exploring my curves with a possessive warmth that left me breathless. His fingers traced down my side, slipping under the hem of my shirt, skimming over my skin making me gasp. His touch was electric, every brush of his hand sparking something deep and undeniable.

Before I knew it, he had lifted me slightly, pulling me into his lap as the kisses grew more fevered, his hands roaming over me as though he couldn't get enough. My heart pounded as he kissed down my neck, his lips warm and firm against my skin, leaving a trail of heat that made me arch into him. His hands slipped lower, teasing and exploring, his touch sending waves of anticipation through me.

He moved lower, his hands slipping to my hips, pulling me closer as he left a trail of kisses down my body, each one making me ache for more. I felt the gentle shift of the boat beneath us, but all I could focus on was the sensation of his mouth, his touch, the way he made me feel like I was the only woman in the world.

After our impromptu boat ride, we strolled into town, walking down Water Street as the late afternoon sun cast a golden glow over everything. Jamal's eyes sparkled with recognition as we passed some of the old shops, and he nudged me, pointing to the recently remodeled *Rewind Rentals*.

"Oh, man," he said, laughing as he shook his head. "I used to come here every Tuesday for Dollar Movie Night. My dad would bring me, and we'd pick out some cheesy action movie or a cartoon—he never said no, even when I wanted to rewatch the same one a hundred times."

"Dollar Tuesday?" I asked, grinning. "Sounds like the highlight of the week."

"Oh, it was the best," he said, his voice full of nostalgia. "I'd spend forever in there, holding up the line, trying to decide between *Space Wars* and some random superhero movie. Eventually, my dad started bribing me with candy from the counter if I'd make up my mind faster."

I laughed, picturing a young Jamal, wide-eyed at the shelves of tapes, torn between galaxies and superheroes. "So you were the kid holding up the line?"

"Guilty," he admitted, raising his hands in mock surrender. "But come on—big choices, you know? Those were the days before streaming. The right pick could make or break your week."

I bumped him playfully with my shoulder. "So, what was your go-to?"

He thought for a second, a smile tugging at his lips. "Always came back to *Galaxy Defenders*," he said, shaking his head as if he were both embarrassed and proud. "I could quote that thing start to finish."

"Really?" I smirked. "Well, you're going to have to prove it sometime. I want to hear the whole thing —action sequences, sound effects, the works."

Jamal chuckled, nudging me back. "Oh, you don't know what you're asking for. But... I'll consider it. Maybe I'll even let you pick the movie next time."

The warmth in his voice and the easy way we joked made me feel close, as if we'd spent years sharing stories like this.

We passed *The Sunflower*, Coral Cove's flower shop, and I slowed down, admiring the bouquets and lush greenery arranged in the window. I'd always loved this shop, with its cozy brick facade and wild tangles of plants displayed out front. Jamal noticed, grinning as he gently tugged my hand and led me through the door.

Inside, the air smelled sweet and earthy, filled with the fragrance of fresh blooms and a hint of vanilla from the candles burning on the counter. I took a deep breath, inhaling the floral scent, feeling instantly at home.

"Serena! Oh, it's so good to see you." Lillian, the shop owner, emerged from behind a display of sunflowers, her face lighting up with a warm smile. Her long dark hair was pulled back with a bright scarf, and she wore a pair of overalls covered in tiny embroidered flowers. "And who's this handsome fellow?"

"This is Jamal," I said, smiling as I introduced him. "He's visiting town, and I thought I'd show him around."

Lillian's eyes sparkled with mischief as she nodded approvingly. "Well, well, Jamal, you've got yourself a gem here." She winked, her hands on her hips. "Now, what can I get you two lovebirds?"

Jamal's face lit up, his gaze turning to the bouquets on display. "Actually, I was thinking I'd pick up some flowers," he said, glancing at me with a smile that made my heart flutter. "For her."

I felt my cheeks warm as Lillian beamed, clapping her hands. "A man with good taste. Let's see..." She bustled over to a display, lifting a bouquet of wildflowers—daisies, lavender sprigs, and tiny sunflowers mixed with greenery. "How about this one? These are some of my favorites, and they look like they're meant for her."

Jamal nodded, taking the bouquet and handing

it to me with a soft smile. "Perfect," he said, his voice gentle as he looked into my eyes. "It suits you."

I took the bouquet, overwhelmed by the simple gesture. "Thank you," I whispered, my heart full as I looked down at the flowers, feeling like I was in some kind of wonderful dream.

Lillian watched us with a knowing smile, leaning on the counter. "Well, you two enjoy your day," she said with a wink. "And Serena, if he knows what's good for him, he'll keep bringing you flowers."

Jamal chuckled, giving her a nod. "I think that's a tradition I can handle."

We said our goodbyes and stepped back outside, the flowers in my hand feeling like a tangible reminder of this magical day. Jamal held my hand as we strolled back down Water Street, and in that moment, I couldn't remember the last time I'd felt this completely and utterly happy.

"Here," he said, nodding toward a small café on the corner. "How about a quick coffee break?"

We settled at a cozy little table, sipping our drinks as he asked about my day-to-day life, my friends, and family. Every question was thoughtful, every response filled with genuine interest. He listened like no one else ever had, and I found myself sharing parts of myself I didn't often reveal, laughing at memories I hadn't thought of in years.

"So, if you could do anything," he asked, leaning forward, his eyes never leaving mine, "no limits, no rules… what would it be?"

The question surprised me, and I took a moment to think about it. "I'd travel the world," I said eventually. "Go somewhere new every month, get lost in cities, explore tiny towns, try all the food. You know… live the life I always talk about but never really go after."

Jamal smiled, his gaze warm. "I can see that. You've got this adventurous spirit—you shouldn't hide it." He reached across the table, his fingers brushing mine. "Maybe one day, we'll take that trip together."

His words settled over me, filling me with an impossible hope that this day—this version of my life—could stretch on forever.

As evening settled, we made our way back to my apartment, and he walked me up the steps, his hand resting on the small of my back. The day had been nothing short of magical, and every moment had felt effortless, natural.

When we reached the door, he hesitated, his eyes meeting mine with an intensity that made my breath catch. "Can I come in?" he asked softly.

I nodded, stepping aside to let him in. My heart raced as I closed the door behind us, the cozy warmth of the apartment wrapping around us as we entered. Jamal took my hand, leading me to the couch, where we sat, our shoulders brushing as we settled into a comfortable silence.

He looked over at me, his gaze softening. "Today was... amazing. I'm glad I got to spend it with you."

"Me too," I whispered, feeling the weight of the day settle in my chest.

Slowly, he leaned closer, his hand finding its way to my cheek as he pressed his lips to mine in a soft, lingering kiss. His touch was gentle, unhurried, and I felt myself melt into him, the warmth of his hand on my skin grounding me, anchoring me to this moment.

One kiss led to another, each one deeper and more intoxicating than the last, and soon we were tangled together, hands roaming, breaths mingling as we lost ourselves in each other.

When we finally pulled back, his forehead rested against mine, our breaths mingling in the quiet of the room. "I don't want this day to end," he murmured, his voice barely above a whisper.

I nodded, my fingers tracing circles on the back of his hand. "Me neither."

We sat in that quiet, intimate space for a long time, savoring each other's presence, holding onto the moment with everything we had.

As he pulled me into his arms on the couch, brushing his fingers through my hair. "This feels like a dream," he whispered, his voice a soft rumble against my ear. "Being here with you."

I looked up, meeting his gaze, the sincerity in his eyes making my heart ache in the best way. "I know," I murmured. "I feel the same way."

He smiled, his thumb tracing gentle circles on the back of my hand, as if savoring every touch. "If this is a dream, I don't ever want to wake up."

We stayed like that, wrapped in each other's warmth. As I drifted off, I allowed myself to hope—just for a moment—that this alternate life with Jamal was real, that tomorrow I'd wake up still wrapped in his arms, with the promise of many more days like this to come.

But when I opened them again, everything was wrong.

CHAPTER 5
Serena

The smell of sugar and peppermint oil filled my nose as I blinked awake. It took me a second to recognize my surroundings: the familiar pastel walls of *Rainbow Bites*, the candy jars lining the shelves, and Zuri hovering over me, her face a mix of concern and intrigue.

"Serena?" she asked, her voice both a question and a lifeline.

I sat up, taking in my surroundings, still feeling the phantom warmth of Jamal's arms around me. My heart fluttered with the memory, but the sudden shift back to reality left me dizzy and disoriented. *How could it feel that real?*

"Wow," I whispered, my voice hoarse with awe. "Zuri... you were right."

Zuri let out a sigh of relief, leaning against the counter as she crossed her arms. "You've been out for like… I don't know, five minutes. What happened? I mean, look at you; you're glowing!"

A soft laugh escaped me, still more disbelief than joy. "It was amazing, Zuri. I thought you undersold it, but now… now I get it." I searched her face, wondering how to put into words the experience, the sheer magic, of waking up in a world where Jamal and I were together. "I was in my own apartment, but it was… different. And Jamal—he was there, and it was like we'd spent a thousand mornings like that."

Zuri's eyes sparkled with excitement. "Oh my gosh, Jamal, as in the cute guy who was here at the boat school? Spill! Was it romantic? Did you guys… you know…" She trailed off, a mischievous grin spreading across her face.

I nudged her, laughing. "No, I mean kinda? But its not just that. We were so close… and it felt so natural, like I'd known him forever. We had this whole day together. There was a boat ride, flowers, the beach, everything. And I just… I didn't want it to end."

Zuri let out a dreamy sigh, her gaze softening as she listened. "That sounds incredible. Like… that's movie magic right there. I didn't think the candy could be that powerful."

"Neither did I." I shook my head, still trying to process it. "It's crazy, right? How could candy make a day feel so real?"

She shrugged, her eyes twinkling. "Maybe it's Coral Cove magic—or maybe it's just a crazy gift from Mrs. Claudette. But whatever it is, it sounds like it's giving us exactly what we need."

I couldn't help but smile, feeling a renewed appreciation for the whimsical magic of this town. "Only in Coral Cove, right?"

"Exactly." She leaned against the counter, glancing around the shop with a wistful smile. "I missed this place, you know. All the little quirks and people who make it feel like home."

We shared a comfortable silence, letting the quiet hum of the shop wash over us. It felt good to be here, in the familiar space we'd both grown up in. Rainbow Bites had seen us through childhood and teenage years, and now, here we were, sharing memories and magic in the very same place.

Just then, the door chimed, and in walked none other than the one and only Jamal.

My heart skipped a beat, and Zuri's eyes went

wide. "Is that…?" she whispered, glancing between Jamal and me.

"Yep," I breathed, feeling a rush of excitement and nerves.

He looked around, clearly taking in the shop with a sense of familiarity, then spotted us and grinned. "Hey, Zuri, Serena," he said my name with a deep purr as he waved, strolling up to the counter with an easy confidence that made my stomach flip.

"Jamal, hi!" I managed, my voice just barely steady as I tried to keep the smile from turning into a full-on grin.

He looked down at the rows of chocolates and candies with a nostalgic smile. "I had to stop by. Every time I'm in town, I make it a point to grab some of these chocolates—best in Coral Cove."

Zuri nudged me with a subtle smile. "She'll get those for you," she said, stepping back and pretending to be busy with some imaginary task behind the counter.

I shot her a grateful glance, then turned back to Jamal, who was now giving me a curious look. "So, you're visiting?"

"Yeah, just for a few days," he replied, leaning casually against the counter. "I went to the boat school, you know, but moved away for work. It's nice to be back. Brings back a lot of memories."

I felt a surge of courage, my fingers lightly brushing the display as I arranged a small box of his favorite chocolates. "Well, I'm glad you stopped by. It's always good to see a familiar face."

He smiled, that warm, easy grin that seemed to make the whole room brighter. "Same here. Coral Cove has a way of pulling people back, huh?"

Zuri suddenly cleared her throat, giving me a pointed look. "You know, Serena, sometimes the universe puts opportunities right in front of you. Be a shame to miss one." She grinned, turning her back to us with a barely-contained smirk.

I shot her a quick glare before looking back at Jamal, who was watching me with an amused glint in his eye. "Is she always like that?"

I laughed, feeling a little more at ease. "Only when she thinks she's being helpful."

"Well, I'd say she has a point," he replied, leaning in just a little closer. "Serena, would you like to get dinner with me tonight? I know a spot... if you're free, of course."

My heart raced as I tried to keep my cool. "I'd love to," I replied, unable to stop the smile that spread across my face. "Golden Chopsticks? Say, seven?"

"Read my mind," he said, his voice warm and confident.

He gave us both a wave and left with his chocolates, the bell above the door chiming softly behind him. As soon as he was out of earshot, I turned to Zuri, my face practically glowing.

"You're going on a date!" she squealed, wrapping me in a quick hug. "The universe just handed you a chance to be with him. Don't waste it, okay?"

I nodded, feeling a rush of excitement mixed with nerves. "Okay. I won't."

Later that evening, I stood in front of the mirror, giving myself one last once-over before heading out. Zuri peeked in, giving me an approving nod. "Just thought I'd pop by and wish you good luck," she said. "You look amazing. Now go knock his socks off."

With a final boost of confidence, I made my way to Golden Chopsticks, my heart racing as I spotted Jamal waiting by the door. He looked up, his face breaking into a smile when he saw me. "Hey, you."

"Hey yourself," I replied, feeling warmth spread through me as he took my hand. His touch was steady and sure, and the thrill of his fingers against mine sent a flutter to my stomach.

As we settled into a cozy corner booth, the dim lighting wrapped us in a comfortable intimacy. The clinking of glasses and quiet chatter of other diners faded as he looked across the table at me, his gaze soft but filled with a curious spark.

"So," he started, leaning forward with an easy smile. "What's it like being in Coral Cove? You seem like someone who really belongs here."

I laughed, running a finger along the edge of my glass. "It's just home, you know? I grew up here, so I guess I'm used to all the little quirks. But having Zuri back has made me see it with fresh eyes. Sometimes, you forget the charm of a place until someone else reminds you."

He nodded, his eyes never leaving mine. "I get that. Coral Cove definitely has a kind of magic. And I can see why you've stayed; it suits you."

As we spoke, I felt his foot brush against mine under the table, the accidental touch lingering just a second longer than necessary. He didn't pull away, and neither did I. Instead, I nudged him back, a silent, playful challenge. He raised an eyebrow, a grin tugging at the corners of his mouth, accepting the game.

"So," he said, his voice dropping slightly as he held my gaze, "if you could do anything, anywhere… what would it be?"

The question made me pause, and I felt a rush of excitement bubbling up at the thought. "I'd travel. See the world, get lost in new cities, taste every kind of food out there. Just… live fully. No rules."

He chuckled, nodding in approval. "No rules, huh? That sounds like trouble."

"Good trouble," I corrected, winking. "The best kind."

Our feet brushed again, this time more deliberate. I felt the warmth of his foot pressing lightly against mine, and my heart raced. Each touch sent a little thrill up my leg, a reminder that this was real, that he was right here.

He leaned in, resting his chin on his hand as his fingers played idly with the edge of his napkin. "And where would you go first? Paris, Tokyo, Rome?"

"Hm…" I tapped my chin, pretending to consider. "Paris is a classic, but I think I'd start somewhere unexpected. Maybe… a road trip down the coast? Stop in every little seaside town and see what secrets they hold."

He let out a soft laugh, shaking his head in admiration. "I like that. Guess I'll have to brush up on my spontaneous road trip skills."

"Oh, so you'd come with me?" I teased, giving him a playful look.

He leaned closer, his voice dropping to a murmur. "Maybe I would."

The air between us grew charged, his gaze steady on mine, and I felt a heat rise in my cheeks. The brush of his foot against mine became a light press, like a silent promise. My hand, resting on the table, found its way closer to his, and when our fingers brushed, he wrapped his around mine, his touch warm and grounding.

We both looked down at our entwined hands, the silence between us filled with more than words could express. Finally, he looked back up, his gaze softened by the faintest hint of vulnerability. "I have to admit," he said, his voice barely above a whisper, "I didn't expect this."

"Expect what?" I asked, my heart pounding.

"This connection," he replied, his thumb brushing over my knuckles, sending a thrill through me. "It feels… effortless. Like I've known you forever."

I bit my lip, the truth sitting heavy on my heart. "Me too," I whispered, my voice shaky. "It's strange, but… good. Really good."

We stayed that way for a moment, lost in each other, the sounds of the restaurant fading into the background. When he finally let go of my hand, his fingers lingered, the heat of his touch staying with me even as he reached for his drink.

"Okay, next question," he said, his eyes twinkling. "What's the craziest thing you've ever done?"

I laughed, pretending to think about it. "Honestly? Probably running out of here tonight to catch up with you."

He grinned, clearly pleased. "Good to know I rank high on your list of wild decisions."

"Oh, trust me, you're right at the top," I teased, nudging his foot with mine again, feeling bolder than ever.

The rest of the dinner passed in a blur of laughter, lingering touches, and shared glances that said more than words. When the night finally came to an end, he offered me his hand, helping me up from the table. The moment his fingers closed around mine, I knew I'd never forget this night.

Outside, under the soft glow of streetlights, he walked me back to my apartment, his fingers laced with mine. As we reached my door, he turned to face me, his eyes searching mine, a gentle smile playing at his lips.

"Thank you for tonight," he murmured, his voice full of warmth.

I smiled, feeling a flutter in my chest. "Thank you," I replied, my heart full as I leaned up and pressed a soft kiss to his cheek.

As he pulled away, his fingers gave mine one last squeeze, and he walked off into the night, leaving me standing on my doorstep, grinning like a love-struck teenager.

CHAPTER 6

Zuri

Rainbow Bites was quiet this afternoon, the usual hum of customers replaced by the soft crackling of the overhead lights. Sunlight poured through the large front windows, casting gentle hues across the colorful jars and shelves. I leaned against the counter, watching Serena as she moved through the shop, her eyes bright with excitement.

"So you're telling me," I said slowly, a grin tugging at the corners of my mouth, "that you and Jamal took a boat ride, got flowers, and ended the night in some epic romance-novel-worthy goodbye?"

Serena leaned back, crossing her arms, a

dreamy smile lighting up her face. "Yes! I can still hardly believe it. Zuri, it was… it was like magic. And he's just as sweet and funny in real life as he was in that candy world. He's everything I ever wanted."

I couldn't help but laugh, but there was a warmth in my chest that wasn't just from the sugary air. Seeing Serena so thrilled, so completely herself, reminded me of how deeply we were connected— even after all the little arguments, the teasing, and the phases where we couldn't understand each other at all. She'd always been my anchor, and in this moment, I was so proud of her.

"I'm happy for you," I said sincerely, reaching over to squeeze her hand. "You deserve this, Serena. You deserve all the love and happiness in the world."

Serena's gaze softened as she looked at me, and for a moment, I saw a flicker of something unreadable in her eyes—like she could sense the swirling thoughts beneath my smile. She tilted her head, her fingers tracing the edge of a candy jar thoughtfully.

"What about you, though?" she asked, her voice gentle. "Didn't you say Brandon was in your candy dream? That must've been… intense."

The question hit a bit closer to home than I'd expected. I glanced away, fiddling with a stray piece of wrapping paper on the counter. "Yeah, it was intense," I admitted, my voice barely above a whisper. "It felt so real—like I was reliving a part of my life I'd left behind, but I wasn't... I wasn't the me I thought I was."

Serena frowned, inching closer. "What do you mean? Was it a good kind of intense or... something else?"

I took a deep breath, gathering the courage to say what had been gnawing at me since I'd woken up from that alternate reality. "In that world, I was... different. And not in a good way. I was cheating on Brandon, and I didn't even seem to care. It's like I was living this whole life I'd never choose for myself. I felt like a stranger, Serena, like I couldn't trust myself."

Her brow furrowed as she reached across the counter, taking my hands in hers. "Zuri, that's not who you are. You're one of the most loyal, genuine people I know. If that candy showed you some alternate version of yourself, it doesn't mean that's who you're meant to be."

"But what if it is?" The words tumbled out before I could stop them. "What if that's just... me, deep down? Not enough for anyone. Not built for commitment or stability or whatever it is people look for in relationships."

Serena squeezed my hands, her expression soft but unwavering. "Zuri, stop. You're not defined by one dream—one version of yourself that isn't even real. You're thoughtful and kind, and you put your whole heart into everything you do. You took over this shop, didn't you? You make people feel loved and welcome every single day, even if it's just through a handful of gummy bears."

A small smile crept onto my face despite the tears pricking at my eyes. "But being the 'Queen of Sweets' isn't the same as being in a relationship. Maybe I'm just not cut out for that."

"Zuri." Her voice was gentle, yet full of conviction. "Everyone has their insecurities, but you're putting way too much pressure on yourself. None of us are perfect. The right person is going to see all of you, insecurities and all, and love you for exactly who you are."

The knot in my chest began to loosen, just a little. I took a shaky breath, letting her words settle in. "It's just… hard to believe sometimes. Especially after seeing myself like that."

Serena leaned back, crossing her arms with a

playful smile. "Well, you know what I think? I think you deserve someone who can show you that love isn't about being perfect. It's about being real, flaws and all. Someone who makes you feel comfortable enough to be exactly who you are, even on the bad days."

I raised an eyebrow, amused by her subtle hint. "Like Jake, you mean?"

A mischievous glint sparkled in her eyes. "Maybe! He seems to bring out a different side of you—one that's confident and relaxed. And have you noticed the way he looks at you?"

I laughed, feeling my cheeks flush. "Okay, okay, maybe I have noticed. But it still feels scary. I don't want to mess things up before they even start."

"Look," Serena said, resting a hand on my shoulder, "you don't have to have it all figured out right now. Take things one step at a time. Enjoy the little moments, trust yourself, and let someone love you for all the things you think you need to fix."

A warmth blossomed in my chest, her words settling over me like a blanket on a chilly evening. "Thanks, Serena. I needed to hear that."

"Anytime," she replied, pulling me into a hug. "You're going to be okay, Zuri. You're enough, just as you are."

As I hugged her back, the weight of my self-doubt lifted just a little. The candy had shown me one version of myself, a version that wasn't perfect—but Serena reminded me that maybe I didn't need to be.

CHAPTER 7

Zuri

Even after hearing Serena's heartfelt words and listening to her stories of an incredible day with Jamal, I couldn't shake the image of my alternate self with Brandon—how I'd betrayed him, how hollow and confusing it had felt. My fears clung to me like a shadow. But as I sat alone in my small, quiet living room, I held the box of Frosted Sugar Charms. Reverently, I opened it. Is it possible that these show real life? Or is it just a wicked manifestation of our fears?

Serena saw Jamal, and things seemed to go great for her. So why was my trip down candy lane so terrifying? The candy's smooth, frosty surface pressed against my palm, I felt a glimmer of hope.

My phone pinged with a message.

. . .

Jake Bennet: Hey Zuri, I hope you're having a good night.

Zuri: Hey Jake, what's up?

Jake: Do you have breakfast plans? I was thinking you, me, and that little place by the sea?

Zuri: See you at 7am?

Jake: It's a date.

My stomach fluttered at his messages. Maybe, just maybe, if I took a second candy, it would reveal something better—something real. Something like Serena had.

I closed my eyes, took a deep breath, and let the candy melt on my tongue. It tasted like dreams and honey, warm and slightly tangy. The familiar haziness swept over me, pulling me away from Coral Cove. My living room blurred into shimmering golden light, and then...

As the golden light faded, I blinked, adjusting to the dim, fluorescent glow of an office space. The hum of machinery and the faint, metallic scent of chocolate greeted me, tugging at memories of long shifts, late nights, and the high, rigid walls of my life before Coral Cove. I was standing in a sprawling kitchen, surrounded by stainless steel counters and shelves lined with gleaming tools and tempered chocolate, but everything felt cold, almost sterile. The familiar sound of heels clicking across the floor sent a chill up my spine.

"Zuri, finally," a clipped voice snapped. I turned to see Greta DuBois, the head chocolatier I'd worked under for years. Her expression was as sharp as ever, eyes narrowed as she scanned the tray of truffles in front of her. "These truffles are over-tempered. Again."

A knot twisted in my stomach. "I followed the instructions exactly, Greta," I replied, forcing a level tone.

Her lip curled as she leaned closer, inspecting each truffle as if it personally offended her. "Exactly wrong, clearly. I told you to add more cream to the mix this time. Why do you always have to make things difficult?"

Always my fault. No matter how hard I worked, no matter the late hours or effort, it was never enough. In Coral Cove, I ran my own shop, a place where I got to make all the choices. Here, every little decision was subject to scrutiny and correction. I could feel my heart beating faster, frustration boiling beneath the surface.

Greta raised her brows, tapping her finger against the counter. "Well? Are you going to stand there gawking, or are you going to fix it?"

I nodded numbly, stepping forward to take the tray of truffles. "Yes, of course, Greta."

"'Yes, of course, Greta,'" she mimicked with an eye roll, already turning her back on me. "Sometimes I wonder why I ever took you on."

The remark stung, but I swallowed it, feeling the familiar weight of helplessness press down on me. I'd wanted this, hadn't I? This was my dream—to learn from the best, to be in the heart of the industry. But now, standing here under Greta's scrutinizing gaze, the thrill was gone. This wasn't passion or art; it was routine, soulless.

Hours passed in a haze of repetitive tasks, each punctuated by Greta's constant criticism. Every truffle, every batch of caramel, every dusting of cocoa powder seemed to trigger some new dissatisfaction.

By mid-afternoon, I was knee-deep in chocolate shavings, trying to rescue a batch of pralines that had been slightly overcooked. Greta swooped in like a hawk, her lips pursed in a scowl.

"Why are you so slow, Zuri? You're setting us behind schedule."

"I'm working as fast as I can," I said, keeping my tone steady, though my hands were trembling. I could feel the ache in my arms, my back stiff from bending over counters all day. I glanced around the room, at the other chocolatiers who moved in silence, heads down, too afraid to look up and catch Greta's eye.

"Well, if this is your fastest, then maybe you're in the wrong business," Greta sneered, her voice low but laced with enough venom to make me flinch.

The words struck hard, almost physical in their impact. I had once dreamed of becoming her—renowned, respected, running a kitchen with skill and precision. But now, the thought filled me with dread. My mind wandered to Rainbow Bites, to the cozy warmth of the shop, the sense of ownership and creativity that filled every inch of it. I remembered Serena's laughter as she teased me about the new candy displays, the familiar faces of Coral Cove, the way I felt every time I unlocked the doors to start a new day.

Here, there was none of that warmth. Just cold efficiency and constant criticism. And yet, this had once been my goal.

"Zuri!" Greta's voice snapped me back, and I felt her gaze pinning me in place, razor-sharp. "Pay attention. Or is that too much to ask?"

"I'm sorry, Greta," I mumbled, swallowing the frustration that prickled at the edges of my mind.

She shook her head, exasperated. "I don't know why you're wasting your time here if you can't handle the pressure. You're supposed to be a professional."

A sense of detachment washed over me, a strange calm that dulled the sting of her words. I watched Greta, realizing that even in this alternate world, in this long-held dream of being a chocolatier for one of the industry's giants, I was miserable. I wasn't respected. I wasn't even happy.

The day dragged on in this numbing cycle, each moment weighing heavier than the last. By the time my shift was over, I felt hollowed out, a shell of myself. Exhausted, I hung up my apron, trying to brush off the lingering tension as I left the kitchen.

Outside, the streets were quiet, the sky bruised with the purples and deep oranges of sunset. I stood there, staring up at the fading light, feeling a pang of emptiness that I couldn't shake. Somewhere, in some other reality, I was back in Coral Cove, surrounded by warmth and love, with people who believed in me. Here, I was just another worker, a nameless cog in a faceless machine, grinding away in the shadow of someone else's dreams.

Suddenly, all those lingering worries I'd had about getting bored in Coral Cove felt laughable. Boredom was nothing compared to this emptiness, this gnawing sense of dissatisfaction. The thought of returning to the candy shop, to my little corner of joy in Coral Cove, filled me with an aching kind of yearning.

I thought of Serena, of how she'd encouraged me to take this leap and open Rainbow Bites, how she'd been there through all the messy first months of learning the ropes. I thought of the kids' wide-eyed wonder when they walked into the shop, of the couples who bought chocolates as little love tokens.

Here, I was simply surviving. But in Coral Cove,

I was thriving, making something that was something I was proud of.

I closed my eyes, breathing in the cool night air, and let the reality sink in. Maybe this hadn't been a mistake—maybe I'd needed to come here to finally understand what happiness really looked like for me. The dreams I'd once held so close felt brittle now, like old photographs that had faded with time. Coral Cove was more than enough for me. It was my place, my people, my home.

When I opened my eyes, the familiar comfort of my living room greeted me. The warmth of Coral Cove wrapped around me, the sounds of the ocean outside my window, the gentle hum of life settling back in.

I held the empty candy box in my hands, I'd used to bring home a single Frosted Sugar Charm. My heart was full in a way it hadn't been before. This wasn't just about a choice between Coral Cove and some glamorous career—it was a choice to love myself enough to follow what truly made me happy, to let go of the old dreams that no longer served me. I had a shop, a sister, friends, and a budding possibility with Jake that was as real as anything I could imagine. And that, I realized, was more than enough.

CHAPTER 8
Zuri

The morning sun was barely skimming the rooftops as I stepped onto the street, my heart pounding with anticipation. My phone buzzed, and Jake's message was like a gentle reminder of why I'd taken the plunge back into Coral Cove life. After two horrible candy experience, his invitation for breakfast at Joe's Coffee had felt like a lifeline to something real.

When I arrived, Jake was already there, leaning against the weathered doorframe of Joe's, looking at ease in his navy-blue hoodie and jeans. He gave me a smile that was a mixture of warmth and playfulness, and I felt my nerves fade a little.

"Good morning," he greeted, holding the door open for me as we stepped inside the cozy café.

We ordered our breakfast—a pair of loaded bagels and coffees—and after a few minutes, made our way out to the pier, our steps soft on the wood as the town slowly came to life around us. The gentle lapping of water and the warmth of the rising sun created a perfect setting, and as we sat on a bench overlooking the water, it felt like a quiet little world made just for us.

"It's nice being back here with you," Jake said, breaking the comfortable silence. "You know, this place hasn't changed much since high school."

I laughed, taking a sip of my coffee. "You're telling me. I think I've changed more than Coral Cove has."

He chuckled, nodding in agreement. "Yeah, but I think we're both part of the charm here. I mean, who else could run Rainbow Bites better than you?"

I shook my head, smiling. "You're right about that. And you're part of it too. I can't believe how much Rewind Rentals has changed with Amelia and Flynn turning it into a theater. The place has so much more life now."

Jake's expression softened. "Yeah, Amelia has really brought it back to life. And Flynn's ideas are something else. Rewind always felt like a family project, but now it feels like a whole new adventure."

"Must be nice working there," I said, studying his face as he spoke of his family.

He smiled, a little sheepish. "It is. But, believe it or not, I spend most of my time down at the marina, helping with boat rentals, the boat school, and basicly anything else boat related. Rewind's kind of like a family reunion now. My grandparents started it, and I love seeing Amelia carry that legacy. But out on the water... that's where I really feel at home."

There was a sincerity in his voice, a calmness that made me feel steady, too. We shared memories from high school, and it was amazing how naturally he fit into Coral Cove's picture. Talking about the past felt easy with him, like rediscovering a familiar song.

He looked down, brushing his thumb over the edge of his coffee cup. "You know, Zuri... I never thought I'd end up back here. I wanted the adventure, the big city, like everyone else. But coming home? It's been better than I ever thought it'd be."

I nodded, feeling a little twinge of understanding. "I get it. I thought I wanted that too, and I tried to make it work. But Coral Cove has a way of calling us back, doesn't it?"

"Yeah," he said, looking over at me with an intensity that made my stomach flip. "It really does. And I feel like... there's more to stay for now."

The ease between us was warm, but as we sat there, his words stirred something deeper in me, something that wanted to believe I could let my guard down. Jake was steady, familiar, and I could sense he was ready for something real.

"You've always been that guy everyone trusts," I said, looking down at my hands as I spoke. "You're... dependable. And that's rare."

He laughed softly. "I don't know if I'm all that, but thanks. I just know what I want, and I'm finally ready to go for it."

"Even if it's right here in Coral Cove?" I asked, only half-joking, and he nodded without hesitation.

"Especially here," he replied, his gaze never leaving mine. "I've had my fill of temporary things. I want something real."

The word *real* seemed to hang between us, its weight both thrilling and terrifying. A hint of my usual doubts bubbled up, the ones that kept me at arm's length from anything too close, too genuine. The familiar thoughts rose—the fear that maybe I wasn't built for this kind of love, the kind that stays steady through all of life's tides.

What if I let myself believe in something, in someone, only for it to unravel? The memory of my alternate self with Brandon lingered like a shadow, her mistakes and betrayals echoing as reminders of what I feared I could become. What if I hurt someone as deeply as she did? Or worse, what if I turned out to be the one who ended up hurt, left with nothing but regrets and questions?

Maybe that's why keeping a safe distance had always seemed... easier. I could let people close enough to know me but never close enough to rely on me, to need me in the way real love required. Real love wasn't neat and tidy; it was messy and beautiful and fragile. And as much as I wanted it, a part of me feared I'd ruin it the moment I tried.

Jake's eyes softened, as though he could see through the layers of armor I'd built up, right to the raw, vulnerable part of me I kept hidden.

"Hey," he said gently, his voice softening, "you okay?"

I nodded, but it felt more like a reflex than an answer. "Yeah, just... I guess it's hard sometimes, you know?" I tried to push past my hesitations, swallowing back the uncertainty that always seemed to lurk beneath the surface. "I just... it's hard to know if I'm the right kind of person for all this. Sometimes I wonder if I'm really cut out for something lasting." I glanced away, watching the gentle ripple of the water as if it held answers I couldn't find in myself.

Jake didn't say anything right away; he just let the silence settle between us, his gaze steady, giving me space to collect my thoughts. That was one thing about him I already knew I appreciated—he didn't rush me, didn't push for words I wasn't ready to say.

After a moment, I took a shaky breath, letting a few more of my fears slip out. "I think... I don't know, maybe I'm just afraid of what it would mean to really let someone in. I know how to be independent, to take care of myself, but letting someone be part of all that? It's like... what if it all just falls apart? What if I'm not... enough?"

Jake reached over, his hand warm and reassuring on mine. "Zuri," he said softly, "I think you're exactly the kind of person who deserves something lasting. We both are."

His confidence, his steady belief in us, felt like an anchor, grounding me in a way I hadn't expected. I wanted to believe him, to let go of all the walls I'd built up for protection, but it was hard to shake the weight of my own doubts. The worries still lingered, fragile and persistent: that I'd stumble, or that the past would repeat itself, that I'd somehow fall short.

Jake's thumb brushed over the back of my hand, a small, comforting gesture that felt like a promise, and I felt my shoulders ease, just a bit. His presence, so warm and genuine, was a balm to the restlessness in me, a reminder that maybe—just maybe—it was okay to let someone else in, to trust that things could be different this time.

As I looked up at him, those familiar insecurities started to fade, slipping into the background. His gaze held a warmth that seemed to say he saw me, all of me, and wasn't the least bit afraid. And that gave me hope—a fragile, flickering hope—that maybe I could learn to see myself the same way he did.

"Thank you," I whispered, meeting his gaze.

"Anytime," he said softly, a smile tugging at his lips.

The sun was fully up now, casting a golden glow across the water as we sat together, and I felt a warmth blooming inside me, something that felt more real and more possible than anything I'd felt in a long time.

As we got up to leave, he paused, turning to face me. "Would it be okay if I kissed you?"

I barely had time to nod before he closed the small distance between us, his hand finding its way to the small of my back, his fingers pressing gently but firmly. He pulled me in, his gaze holding mine for a heartbeat longer, like he wanted to savor the moment. When his lips finally met mine, it was as if the world around us vanished; his kiss was tender, yet filled with a kind of restrained intensity that took my breath away.

The softness of his lips against mine was a promise, an unspoken vow that felt both thrilling and deeply comforting. His hand slipped from my back to trace the curve of my jaw, his thumb brushing along my cheek as he deepened the kiss, slow and unhurried, as if he had all the time in the world. A shiver ran through me as his fingers threaded through my hair, anchoring me to the moment, grounding me in the warmth of his embrace.

I felt myself melting into him, every fear and hesitation dissolving under the warmth of his touch.

My hands found their way to his chest, fingers curling against the soft fabric of his shirt, and I felt the steady rhythm of his heartbeat beneath my palm, strong and certain. He pulled me even closer, and I could feel his own breath hitch slightly, his pulse quickening, matching the flutter in my chest. It was as if we were both discovering something that had been waiting for this very moment to come alive.

He pulled back just slightly, his forehead resting against mine as he caught his breath, his eyes searching mine with a tenderness that left me feeling both vulnerable and invincible. Then, he leaned in once more, his lips capturing mine in a deeper, more passionate kiss, igniting something inside me that I hadn't felt in years. It wasn't just a kiss; it was a spark, a beginning, a feeling of possibility that seemed to whisper that maybe, just maybe, this was exactly where I was meant to be.

CHAPTER 9
Serena

The morning light filtered softly through the curtains, casting a warm glow over the room where we lay tangled together, our bodies pressed close, his warmth radiating against my skin. Jamal's fingertips traced gentle patterns along my back, sending little shivers down my spine as he pulled me even closer, his breath warm against my ear. I looked up at him, and the smile that spread across his face made my heart skip a beat; there was something in his eyes.

"Hey," he murmured, brushing a strand of hair from my cheek, his voice thick with affection. "I don't think I've ever felt this close to anyone before. You…you're something else, Serena."

His lips found mine, the kiss starting slow, soft,

and then deepening with an intensity that made my pulse race.

My breath hitched as Jamal's hands roamed with practiced ease, slipping beneath my shirt to trace the soft curves of my skin. His lips danced a trail of fire down my neck, sending shivers rippling through me. I felt the weight of his desire, tangible in the air, as he deftly unbuttoned my shirt and peeled it away. His breath was hot against my skin, his tongue tracing a wet path from my collarbone down to the valley between my breasts.

The room spun a little as he knelt before me, his fingers tracing the edge of my jeans before dipping in, teasing. He looked up at me through thick lashes, his intent clear in the darkening of his eyes. With a swift movement, he divested me of my remaining clothes, leaving me exposed and breathing heavily. The cool air of the room played across my heated skin, tightening my nipples into hard peaks that ached for his touch.

As Jamal trailed kisses lower, he paused, the heat of his breath teasing the sensitive skin along my inner thigh. His gaze lifted to meet mine, his eyes shimmering with a mix of desire and deep admiration. He murmured, his voice husky and tender, "You are absolutely exquisite, Serena."

I flushed under his gaze, feeling exposed yet cherished under his intent look. "Jamal," I whispered, my voice catching on his name, overwhelmed by the earnestness in his eyes.

He smiled, his lips brushing against my skin as he spoke, each word a soft caress. "Every curve, every sigh, every response from you is a gift," he continued, his breath warm against my trembling thigh. "Being with you, seeing you unravel like this —it's breathtaking."

His words ignited something fierce and bold within me. "Jamal," I breathed out, my hands finding his shoulders, pulling him closer. "I love how you see me..."

He grinned, then dipped his head lower, his breath now a hot whisper against my most intimate area. "I will worship every inch of you," he declared softly before his tongue resumed its slow, deliberate exploration, his actions matching the promise of his words, leaving me gasping and clutching at him as I surrendered to the sensations he evoked.

Jamal worshipped me with his mouth, kissing and licking my throbbing center. His tongue lapped at me, slow and deliberate, exploring every fold and crevice. I arched into him, gasping as waves of pleasure built up inside me, crashing over me in a relentless tide that left me clutching at his hair, urging him on.

He rose to his full height, his erection pressing insistently against me. With a low growl, he lifted me up effortlessly, my legs wrapping around his waist as he entered me in one fluid motion. I moaned loudly, my back arching as Jamal set a punishing rhythm that drove me wild. He filled me completely, every thrust pushing me closer to the edge. His hands gripped my hips, guiding me to meet each of his thrusts with one of my own.

The coiling tension in my belly wound tighter and tighter, my breaths coming in short, sharp gasps. Jamal's lips found mine in a searing kiss that stole my breath away.

As Jamal moved in a rhythmic dance with me, his breaths heavy and warm against my ear, he whispered fervently between each thrust, "I've never felt this way before, Serena. You've completely captured me."

His words tumbled out in a rush, punctuated by the deep, controlled movements that drew a gasp from me each time. "I'm falling for you," he admitted, his voice thick with emotion as he pulled me even closer, our bodies melding together in the dim light.

With a final, deep thrust, my climax rip through me, my entire body trembling as I clung to Jamal. He followed shortly after, his own release overtaking him as he buried his face in my neck, his body shuddering against mine.

As we caught our breath, wrapped in each other's arms, the connection we shared was rooted in the raw openness and the shared intensity of our lovemaking.

I kissed his forehead. "I've fallen for you too."

CHAPTER 10
Zuri

Lingering in the quiet morning hours of Rainbow Bites, I found myself re-arranging the candy jars—each color coordinated meticulously. It was a Monday, typically slow, with the faint hum of Coral Cove's morning routine just beyond the glass door. Today, Serena was coming in to help; she'd been such a rockstar, stepping in whenever the shop overwhelmed me or I needed a second set of hands.

"Morning, Zuri!" Serena breezed through the door with her usual flair, apron already in hand, a clear sign she was here in more than just the capacity of a visiting sister. "Ready to conquer the candy world?"

I chuckled, nodding towards the register.

"Always. But I'm even more ready to hear about what's been happening with you. Anything you want to share with the class about Jamal and that hicky on your neck?" I arched an eyebrow, a silent prompt for those juicy details sisters just know.

Serena's cheeks flushed a delightful shade of pink, and she leaned in conspiratorially. "Oh my gods, Zuri, it was incredible. I—I actually came twice. It was that good." Her voice dropped to a whisper, and she glanced around like the candy might eavesdrop.

Laughing, I hugged her tight. "I'm so happy for you, really. He sounds like a keeper."

Her smile dimmed as she studied me. "Enough about me. What's going on with you? Something happen with Jake?"

I sighed, resting against the counter. "Yeah, we had breakfast the other morning at Joe's. It was really nice, easy even. Talking to him is so… simple." But as I said it, my thoughts drifted to the bizarre journeys the Frosted Sugar Charms had taken me on—none of which had been simple or easy.

"Simple's good, right? So, what's the 'but'?" Serena knew me too well.

I leaned on the counter, pushing aside a jar of

peppermint twists as Serena looked on, concern etching her features. "It wasn't at all what I expected," I confessed, the weight of the revelation still heavy on my shoulders. "Instead of romance or a perfect alternate life, I saw myself miserable, doing what I once thought was my dream job."

Serena's brow furrowed as she leaned against the counter opposite me. "But you always talked about that job like it was the end-all and be-all of your career dreams. What changed?"

I sighed, fiddling with a candy wrapper. "I know, and that's what scares me. It's like, seeing that life where I followed through with those old dreams —it was nothing like I imagined. I was so unhappy, Serena."

"Unhappy? But why? You were a chocolatier for a major brand, right?" Her tone was a mix of curiosity and gentle probing.

"Yeah, but I was treated poorly, blamed for things out of my control, and jerked around constantly by the boss. It was awful." I shook my head, the bitter taste of disillusionment still lingering. "It made me appreciate this," I gestured around at Rainbow Bites, "so much more. But now I wonder if I'm just settling because I'm scared to chase anything bigger."

Serena reached across the counter, squeezing my hand. "Zuri, maybe the candy isn't showing you what you want, but what you need to see. You've learned something valuable from each trip, even if it's hard."

I pondered her words, the truth in them ringing louder than the bell above our door. "Maybe you're right. Each trip has taught me something... profound about myself. But there's still this nagging feeling, like I'm missing a piece of the puzzle."

"That's why you should try it again," Serena suggested with a hopeful tilt of her head. "One more time could give you the answers you're looking for."

The idea of diving back into the unknown was daunting. Yet, the allure of possibly understanding the persistent feeling of incompleteness was too strong to ignore. "You think so?" I asked, needing the reassurance only a sister could provide.

Serena nodded emphatically. "Absolutely. What's the worst that could happen? You find out more about yourself? That's not a loss, Zuri. That's a win, no matter how you look at it."

Her optimism was infectious, and a small smile crept over my face. "Okay, one last trip," I agreed, reaching for a charm from the box. Holding it between my fingers, I felt the now-familiar mix of apprehension and excitement.

"Go for it, Zuri. I'll be right here, waiting to hear all about it," she encouraged, her voice full of warmth and sisterly support.

With a deep breath, I popped the candy into my mouth, the flavors of vanilla and sea salt a soothing balm as I braced myself for another journey into the possible. As the shop around me began to blur into shimmering light, I held onto Serena's last words, hoping that this final trip would bring the clarity I desperately sought.

The world shifted around me, colors melting into new hues and sounds into unfamiliar tunes as the candy worked its magic, transporting me from the familiar confines of the back room at Rainbow Bites to somewhere entirely different. My eyes fluttered open to a larger, more vibrant version of the candy shop. The walls were adorned with bright, cheerful murals of whimsical landscapes, the shelves brimming with an array of confections that were more exotic and varied than anything I'd ever stocked.

I was standing behind the counter, but this wasn't just any day at the shop; it was the shop's anniversary, and it was bustling with people. Children laughed as they pointed at towering stacks of rainbow lollipops, while adults chatted amiably, holding steaming cups of cocoa topped with whipped cream and a sprinkle of chili powder—a specialty I apparently developed that had become a local favorite.

As I moved through the crowd, greeting customers with ease and a genuine smile, I noticed the framed photos along the wall. There were pictures of me with various groups of friends, at community events, and holiday gatherings, each image radiating warmth and fulfillment. A particularly striking photo caught my eye: it was me at a local charity event, holding a giant check. The caption read, "Rainbow Bites Gives Back."

Turning away from the wall, I made my way to the back of the shop where a small party had been set up. A banner overhead read, "Here's to Many More Sweet Years!" My employees, more like friends in this reality, gathered around, raising glasses in a toast.

"To Zuri, who makes all this possible!" one of them cheered, and the room erupted in applause.

I felt a surge of pride and fulfillment, not from external validation but from the internal recognition of my own capabilities and the happiness that bubbled up from living a life aligned with my values and passions. As the party continued, I mingled, laughing and sharing stories, the ease and comfort of my interactions underscoring a deep-seated confidence and contentment that came from knowing I had built this life on my own terms.

Later, as the guests thinned and the sun began to set, I took a moment to step outside. The shop overlooked a small, serene park, the setting sun casting long shadows on the grass. I walked alone, but there was no loneliness in my steps—only peace. Each stride was a testament to a life well-lived, a life full and rich without the need for someone else to validate my existence or happiness.

As I sat on a park bench, watching families pack up their picnic baskets and kids chase the last rays of daylight, I realized that this vision, this version of life, was teaching me something vital. It wasn't about having someone by my side; it was about the love I had for my own life, the passions I pursued, and the community I nurtured. Love, I understood then, was expansive and varied, and I was already whole without needing to be filled by another.

Slowly, the park scene faded, the laughter and light dissolving as I found myself back in the dimness of the shop's back room. The stark contrast made my lesson even clearer. My heart felt lighter, my purpose more defined. I knew now that my worth wasn't tied to someone else's presence in my life. It was rooted deeply in my own being, in the life I chose every day. With a renewed sense of self, I was ready to face the world—alone or not—with a bold heart and an open spirit.

As I returned to reality, the bell above the shop door jingling as it swung closed behind a customer, a new sense of clarity washed over me. My fears, those nagging doubts about my worth and capability to love, didn't define my ability to be whole. I didn't need to be perfect or fearless to deserve love; I was already deserving, just as I was.

I stepped out from the back room, finding Serena restocking some shelves. She looked up, a questioning smile on her face.

"I'm good," I told her, more to myself than to her, feeling the weight of my past insecurities lifting. "Actually, I'm more than good. I'm ready—ready to live, to love, and to embrace whatever comes my way, without any candy trips."

Serena laughed, coming over to wrap me in a warm embrace. "That's my sister," she said, pride evident in her voice. "You've always been whole,

Zuri. Sometimes, it just takes a little magic to see it."

As she went back to her tasks, I looked around at the little shop that had seen so much of my life unfold. Coral Cove wasn't just a place I lived; it was a part of me, as essential as breathing. With a renewed spirit and an open heart, I was ready to face life head-on, embracing each day with the vigor of someone who truly understood her own worth.

CHAPTER 11
Zuri

The last rays of the afternoon sun glinted off the windows of Rainbow Bites as Jake pulled up in his well-worn truck, a grin spreading across his face as soon as he saw me stepping out. "Ready for an adventure in dining?" he asked, his voice tinged with the excitement that seemed to bubble up so effortlessly between us.

"Always," I replied, sliding into the passenger seat. The scent of the ocean mingled with the faint smell of leather and engine oil, a combination that was quickly becoming a comforting constant in my life. As we drove away from the shop, I turned to him, eager to share the whirlwind of ideas and changes that had consumed me over the past few days.

"I've started repainting the shop," I began, my words tumbling out as I described the new color scheme—bright, hopeful hues that reflected the vibrancy I felt inside. "And I've been reaching out to vendors about those extravagant candy ideas I had. It's like I'm finally bringing the Rainbow Bites of my dreams to life."

Jake listened, his eyes on the road but his attention fully on me. "Sounds like you're really diving into this new vision of yours," he said, a note of admiration in his voice. "What sparked all this sudden inspiration?"

I hesitated, the weight of the secret I'd been carrying pressing on my chest. "Actually, that's part of what I wanted to talk to you about tonight," I said, my fingers nervously playing with the strap of my purse.

We arrived at the restaurant, a cozy little place by the marina with a view of the boats bobbing gently in the harbor. The hostess led us to a quiet table by the window, and as we sat down, the soft glow of the setting sun bathed everything in golden light.

As we ordered our food, I took a deep breath, ready to dive into the depths of my recent experiences. "Jake, there's something I haven't told you about… about how I came to see my life and the shop in a new light."

He leaned forward, his expression open and curious. "I'm all ears, Zuri."

"It's going to sound a bit out there, but… it involves these things called Frosted Sugar Charms," I began, watching his reaction closely.

Jake's interest didn't falter as I ventured further into my explanation. His curious gaze never left my face, a testament to his openness to the peculiar bounds of Coral Cove's mystique, which he was already somewhat familiar with through the bizarre happenings often whispered about around town.

I exhaled, steadying my nerves to reveal the depth of my experiences. "The first few trips were rough, unsettling even. They showed me scenarios where I was living out what I thought were my dreams, but instead, I found dissatisfaction and regret," I explained, the memories vivid enough to stir a discomfort that I tried to keep from my voice.

He nodded slowly, processing my words with a thoughtful frown. "That sounds intense. But it seems like it gave you some clarity, at least?"

"It did," I admitted, a slight smile tugging at the corner of my lips. "The last trip was different. It showed me a life where I wasn't with anyone—no whirlwind romance or partner. But I was happy, thriving even. I was running a version of Rainbow Bites that was all mine, filled with success and personal fulfillment. It was just me, enjoying my life, my work, deeply connected with friends and family."

Jake's expression softened, his hand reaching across the table to cover mine, a gesture of support that sent warmth spreading through me. "Zuri, that's incredible. It sounds like you found what you really needed to see. Something true to who you are and what you value."

Encouraged by his understanding, I took a deep breath before revealing the full extent of my evening's plan. "That's why I brought one of the charms with me tonight," I said, pulling the small candy from my purse and setting it on the table. His eyes widened slightly in surprise.

"You want me to try it?" he asked, a mix of astonishment and intrigue coloring his tone.

I nodded. "I do. I think... if you saw what I've seen, you'd understand me even more. And that's why I brought another charm with me tonight. Not to escape this reality, but to share it with you. There are no secrets between us, and I want you to see this part of my world, Jake. Especially not now, when I feel like everything is finally coming together for me."

He studied the candy for a moment, then looked up at me with a resolve that made my next breath easier to draw. "Alright, Zuri. I trust you. Let's see where this takes me." He picked up the charm, hesitated just a moment as if to savor the precipice of the unknown, and then popped it into his mouth.

Watching him close his eyes, the gentle evening light casting soft shadows across his features, I felt a bond tightening between us—one woven with threads of magic, trust, and the beginning of shared secrets.

As the candy dissolved, his eyes fluttered shut, and a peaceful expression settled over his features. I watched, holding my breath, waiting to see what world he would find himself in—and hoping more than anything that it would bring him back to me with a deeper understanding and connection.

CHAPTER 12
Jake

Opening my eyes, the familiar sensation of my bedroom seemed oddly transformed. The sheets felt softer, and a gentle morning light filtered through curtains I didn't recognize. As I turned to my side, my breath caught—Zuri was there, her hair splayed across the silk pillow, a serene smile on her lips as she slept.

The room spun for a moment as I tried to ground myself in the reality that seemed both mine and not. My heart raced, and I sat up, causing the sheets to rustle. Zuri's eyes fluttered open, and she turned toward me, her smile deepening.

"You okay?" she asked gently, propping herself on one elbow.

"Yeah, I just... I ate one of your candies," I

managed to say, my voice a mix of wonder and disbelief.

She didn't seem surprised; instead, her smile turned mischievous. "And?" she prompted, pulling me closer.

Her touch was electric, sparking memories that felt both implanted and intimate. As I leaned into her kiss, I noticed a large diamond ring on her finger, catching the soft light. Panic and pleasure warred within me as I took in the room around us —photos of us, laughing, holding each other, hanging on the walls. It was a life, our life together, crystallized in frames.

Realization dawned that I was not just in a house, but our home. The intimacy of the space, the personal touches that screamed Zuri yet felt part of me, overwhelmed my senses. We were naked, the remnants of what seemed a night spent in passion still clinging to our skin. Zuri's hands explored, her lips trailing down my chest to my abdomen, each touch reigniting a familiarity that puzzled yet pleased me. She nipped at my neck, sending a jolt of pleasure through me, her breath hot against my earlobe.

Moaning, I reciprocated, my hands finding her breasts, feeling her nipples harden under my touch.

She wriggled, a sound of pure delight escaping her as I switched my attention between her breasts, ensuring each received its share of pleasure.

Her body responded, arching towards me as I explored her with kisses and touches, a deliberate descent to the crescendo of her desire. As my lips traced the line of her stomach, finding the silken heat between her thighs, she was already trembling, a clear sign of her readiness. Her moans filled the room, a symphony to which my actions set the tempo.

I parted her legs further, the intimacy of the moment heightening with every breath. My tongue found her wet pussy, tasting her, drawing circles around her clit until she was clutching at the sheets, her back arching off the bed. Her pleas, a litany of whispered encouragements, spurred me to deepen the exploration, pressing into her warmth with a fervor that promised release.

Entering her felt like a homecoming, our bodies aligning with a rhythm that seemed as ancient as time itself. Each movement was a stroke of heat, building a tension that promised to shatter the calm we had created. She climbed atop me, her movements a dance of passion, each shift bringing us closer to the edge. When her release came, it was a tempest, her cries a song of ecstasy that filled the room, echoing in the silence that followed. My own climax was a beat behind, a rush of sensation that felt like the breaking of a dam.

In the aftermath, the room was silent save for our heavy breathing, a testament to the storm we had weathered together. Our connection—a tapestry woven from threads of desire, trust, and mutual fulfillment—was palpable, a narrative spun from the language of bodies that spoke profoundly of love and longing.

Lying back, spent, her laughter filled the air, light and beautiful. "Do you think we woke the kids up?" she teased, a twinkle in her eye.

The mention of kids—a life so full and complete—sent a wave of contentment through me. She mentioned needing to open Rainbow Bites and asked if I could take the kids to school. "Yes, anything for you, my queen," I responded without hesitation, the words feeling as natural as breathing.

As reality began to pull me back, the restaurant reappeared around me, Zuri watching me with a hopeful, expectant look. I smiled, the memory of our shared life vivid and warming.

"That was… incredible," I said, my voice thick with emotion. "I've never felt anything so real."

"What did you see?" she asked, leaning in, her eyes searching mine.

"You," I answered simply. "I saw us, a whole life filled with love and happiness. I saw what could be."

Her eyes welled up, a hopeful whisper escaping her lips. "Really?"

"Yes," I said, reaching across the table to take her hand, feeling the future in our touch. "I'm in. All in. You, me, whatever comes next."

The kiss that followed was a promise, a seal on the future we both desired. As our lips met, the world fell away, leaving only the certainty of us, the path forward clear and bright.

If you enjoyed **Frosted Sugar Charms**, check out my Tarot Fantasies series!

Nestled in the heart of this quaint town, The Arcane Room is a sanctuary for those seeking a unique blend of magic, mystery, and personal transformation.

As you cross the threshold, the rich scent of sandalwood and exotic spices envelops you, creating an atmosphere of warmth and intrigue. The shop is a treasure trove of New Age paraphernalia—shelves lined with books on magic, tarot, and manifestation, a dazzling array of crystals, and over two hundred varieties of tarot decks. A beacon of the shop's mystical charm is a magnificent amethyst crystal situated at its core.

Your guide through this journey is the enigmatic Ms. Vesper, whose presence is as captivating as the shop itself. With her velvety voice and inviting demeanor, she offers more than just items; she provides experiences. "Welcome," she says, her eyes twinkling with the promise of hidden secrets. "Would you like to see what kind of one-of-a-kind experience I can offer you today?"

Intrigued, you follow Ms. Vesper to a secluded room at the back of the shop. Here, she presents a deck of tarot cards and invites you to draw one, setting the stage for a magical experience like no other. "We offer a unique experience here—a little magic, if you will. It's an exploration of your deepest desires guided by the power of tarot," she explains.

Once you draw a card, the adventure begins. In this enchanted simulation, your chosen card becomes a gateway to a realm where fantasies are brought to life. The experience is not for the faint of heart but for those ready to confront their fears and embrace their desires. As you relax on the luxurious chaise lounge, a warm light envelops you, transporting you to a world that feels more real than reality itself.

Whether you're looking to unlock the secrets of your heart or simply indulge in a bit of magical escapism, The Arcane Room offers an experience that will leave all visitors transformed.

Also by Jax Wilder

Coral Cove Series

Sleighed by Love

Harvesting Love

Dawning Desire

Knead You Now

Love Rewound

Perfect Lover Spell

Haunted by Her

Red, White, and Ravished

Frosted Sugar Charms

Tarot Fantasies Series

The Devil's Temptations

Strength of the Beast

Hanged Passions

Six of Cups

Death's Embrace

Queen of Pentacles

Lorelai Hamilton

About the Author

Jax Wilder is a passionate romance author hailing from a charming small town nestled in the picturesque Pacific Northwest. With a heart full of love and an unyielding belief in the power of happily ever afters, Jax weaves enchanting tales of love and connection that leave readers captivated.

Jax's novels are a reflection of her commitment to celebrating the magic of love, and her characters' journeys mirror the warmth and happiness she has found in her own life. Join her on the enchanting journey of love, passion, and enduring connection through her heartfelt romance novels.